Millie and Bombassa

Make friends with the

funniest duo in town!

 Be sure to read:

Dizzy D.I.Y.!
Cash Crazy!
Holiday Hassle!

... and lots, lots more!

D-Day Disaster!

written and illustrated by
Shoo Rayner

SCHOLASTIC

Scholastic Children's Books,
Commonwealth House, 1-19 New Oxford Street,
London, WC1A 1NU, UK
a division of Scholastic Ltd
London ~ New York ~ Toronto ~ Sydney ~ Auckland
Mexico City ~ New Delhi ~ Hong Kong

First published by Scholastic Ltd, 2003

Copyright © Shoo Rayner, 2003

ISBN 0 439 97857 2

Printed in Singapore

10 9 8 7 6 5 4 3 2 1

The right of Shoo Rayner to be identified as the author
and illustrator of this work has been asserted by him in accordance
with the Copyright, Designs and Patents Act, 1988.

Chapter One

Bombassa woke to a bright and sunny new day.

"What a beautiful day," he said to himself.

He made a huge cup of tea and climbed back into his warm, cosy bed. He opened the biscuit tin and took out two huge biscuits.

He dunked the biscuits in his tea and made crumby, wet splodges all over the duvet as he ate them.

When he'd finished, he stared dreamily out of the window. The sun was shining and the sky was as blue as it could be.

"What a lovely day," he sighed. "What a perfect morning. Tea and biscuits in bed. Just what the doctor ordered. Ha, ha!"

He laughed at his little joke, before he snuggled down and slipped back into a lovely, comfortable doze.

Soon he was fast asleep and dreaming of picnic teas by the river.

But his lovely dream was broken by
something twittering in his ear.

"Wake up, Bombassa!
It's hot and the sun is
shining. You can't
stay in bed on a day
like this. I think we
should do something special."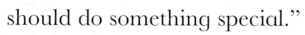

It was Millie, Bombassa's best friend.

Bombassa groaned. He pulled down a little
bit of duvet so he could see the window.
Millie was right. It really was a lovely day.

"Hmmm…" he mumbled.

"I thought we might go to the mall," said Millie.

Bombassa liked the mall. It had some very nice tea shops. "We could go to a tea shop," he said excitedly. "I'd better just check my calendar in case I'm doing something else today."

"I'll do it," said Millie, hopping up on to the shelf. She peered at Bombassa's *Teas of the World* calendar.

"There's nothing special written down for today," she said. "Just the letter D in red ink."

Bombassa was silent. Millie turned to look at him.

Bombassa's eyes were as wide as saucers.

"D-d-d-did you say a letter d-d-d-D in red ink?" he stammered.

Millie looked concerned. "Yes. What does it mean?"

Bombassa groaned, "It's D-day!"

"D-day?" asked Millie. "What's D-day?"

If it had started out a bright, sunny day, it now looked as though a heavy, dark thundercloud had settled over Bombassa's head.

"D-day," he moaned. "It means that Auntie Daz is coming today! She'll go bonkers when she sees this place. Just look at the mess."

"Well," said Millie, who knew very well
how Auntie Daz felt about untidiness.
"We'd better get tidying straight away."

But just as Bombassa was putting on his
dressing gown, the doorbell rang.

The two friends stared at each other in
horror.

The doorbell rang again and the unmistakeable voice of Auntie Daz bellowed through the letterbox.

Chapter Two

Bombassa opened the door a crack and
Auntie Daz barged in.

"I just don't believe it!" she fumed. "It's
eleven o'clock and you're still in your
dressing gown!"

Millie and Bombassa trembled as Auntie Daz examined each untidy room.

"Look at the state of this place!" she went on. "I don't suppose it's been tidied for weeks… I don't suppose you've even got out of bed for weeks!"

Millie thought quickly. "We were planning to spring clean the place. We were waiting for your expert advice." She winked at Bombassa. "Weren't we?"

"Oh … er … um … absolutely! Just as Millie says, we were waiting for you," said Bombassa.

Auntie Daz glowed with pleasure. "Well, you're in luck. I happen to be the world's greatest spring cleaner. We'll have this place looking like new in no time."

She opened her vast handbag and pulled out a pair of pink rubber gloves.

"It's lucky I came prepared," she beamed.

Chapter Three

As soon as Bombassa was dressed, Auntie Daz marched into the kitchen.

"We'll start in here," she yelled as she began emptying the cupboards. "Come along, you two. Start sorting out this mess."

Auntie Daz hustled and bustled.
Dusting and
wiping...

...sweeping...

...and shining.

Every so often, she barked orders at Millie
and Bombassa.

"Take this outside!"

"Put this in the bin!"

"Do something with this!"

"Put that away!"

Auntie Daz cleared out all Bombassa's cupboards and drawers. She put things back exactly where *she* thought they ought to go. She put the table and chairs exactly where *she* thought they ought to be.

"You see," she announced, "it's so much better like this."

Bombassa sighed and threw a tired look at Millie.

Next, Auntie Daz strode into the lounge.
"This room is full of rubbish!" she bellowed.

"Look at this! Old magazines, empty
biscuit tins, empty packets of tea and three
broken radios!"

Bombassa tried to explain. "It's my collection. I collect biscuit tins and tea packets and I'm going to try and mend those radios … one day."

Auntie Daz made Bombassa throw everything away.

He put it all into rubbish sacks, which he stored safely in the shed. He could put everything back when Auntie Daz had gone home.

"I can't stand clutter," Auntie Daz said, emptying a pile of dried-up biros from an old teacup into the bin. "You have a cluttered mind, Bombassa. Clear out the clutter and you will see the world in a fresh, new light."

Bombassa wasn't sure that he wanted to see the world in a fresh, new light. He was hot, bothered and exhausted. He wanted to have a nice cup of tea and go back to bed.

"Now, what's this?" Auntie Daz waved a tall, red tin in front of Bombassa.

Bombassa smiled when he saw it. It had been a present. Once it had been filled with the most delicious biscuits he could ever remember eating.

He'd lost the lid, so it was no use as a tin any more, but he couldn't throw it away. It reminded him of just how delicious biscuits could be!

"It's a vase," he said, thinking quickly.

"Well then," Auntie Daz barked, "put some flowers in it!"

Millie and Bombassa slipped out to the garden to look for some flowers. It was a brief moment of peace.

"She's gone spring-cleaning mad!" said Millie.

"Never mind," Bombassa sighed. "Maybe she'll go home when she's finished. Then I can put everything back where it's meant to be."

They found some flowers, put them in the tin and filled it with water.

"Lovely," said Auntie Daz. "You can put it on the mantelpiece."

"Now," said Auntie Daz excitedly, "look what I found hiding at the back of a cupboard."

She held up a framed photograph of herself.

"I think this would go nicely over the mantelpiece … just above the flowers."

"Oh, that would be really nice," Bombassa
lied, "but I haven't got any nails."
The last thing he
wanted on his
wall was a
photo of
Auntie Daz.

Auntie Daz beamed. "I found some nails
in the back of a drawer. I found a hammer
too. Come along … fetch the stepladder!"

Bombassa was past caring. He was hot and bothered and in terrible need of a cup of tea.

He whacked the nail so hard that it bent.

"Careful!" said Millie. "You could really hurt yourself."

Even though the nail was bent, Bombassa managed to hang the photo on the wall.

"Right!" he said defiantly. "It's time for tea!"

Chapter Four

Nothing was in its normal place.

The kettle was on the wrong side of the kitchen, and it was plugged in where the toaster should have been.

And when Bombassa opened the tea cupboard, there was no tea!

"Hey!" he complained. "Where's the tea gone?"

"I've reorganized everything for you,"
Auntie Daz said, proudly. "Everything is
now in its proper, ordered place. Your life
will be so much more efficient!"

Bombassa banged around the kitchen,
looking for the tea.

At last he found it in a bottom, corner cupboard. "What a stupid place to put it!" he muttered under his breath.

He chose his favourite tea and stood up. He didn't notice that he'd left a cupboard door open above his head.

Bang!

"Ow! Who left that open?" Bombassa
yelled. Slightly dizzy,
he stepped back
and tripped over
a chair that
had never
been there
before.

"Where did that come from?" he croaked,
as he landed hard on his bottom, knocking
over the table that used to be on the other
side of the kitchen.

"What's that doing there?" he cried, as he stumbled through the lounge door, bumping into the bookcase that used to be in the hall. As the bookcase toppled over, Bombassa fell over and a pile of books fell on to his tummy.

"Oof! Where did they come from?" he wheezed.

Angrily, he hurled the books off his
tummy, narrowly missing Millie, who was
trying to help him up.

She leaped into the air and flew to the
first safe place she saw – Auntie Daz's
photo.

But it wasn't as safe as it looked. The nail was bent. It only just held the photo on the wall. It couldn't take Millie's tiny weight as well.

Down came the photo, knocking off the tin of flowers, which landed right on Bombassa's horn.

Auntie Daz ran to help and bumped into the big brass lamp that used to be in the bedroom.

The lamp crashed down on Bombassa's head, knocking him out and squashing the tin firmly on to his horn!

Finally, the photo tipped off the mantelpiece and landed on Bombassa's chest.

Millie noticed a message scrawled on the photo: *To my favourite nephew, with all my love... Auntie Daz xx*

"Oh dear!" whimpered Auntie Daz. "I'd better phone for an ambulance."

Chapter Five

Millie and Auntie Daz went in the ambulance with Bombassa.

When they arrived at the hospital, a very nice ostrich took his pulse and made him say, "Aah!"

The tin was jammed on tight, making it hard to breathe properly.

"Urrgh!" Bombassa spluttered.

The doctor pulled and pushed. Bombassa moaned and groaned. Finally, the tin came off.

The doctor took some X-rays, which showed that Bombassa had a fractured horn. It would have to be set in plaster for a month.

"Stay in bed until you feel better," the doctor told him.

The next day Millie came to visit
Bombassa at home.

"The plaster makes me see everything
double," Bombassa complained. "I can't
walk properly, so I keep bumping into
things. And my bottom aches terribly!"

"It must be awful for you," said Millie.
Just then, the sound of Auntie Daz's singing
drifted up the stairs.

Millie cocked her head towards the noise. "So she's still here, then?"

"Yes!" said Bombassa, brightening up. That's the only good thing. She's staying until P-day."

Millie looked confused. "P-day?"

Bombassa nodded at the calendar.

"That's the day my plaster comes off. Until then I have to stay in bed and Auntie Daz is going to look after me."

He picked up
a small bell
and rang it.
"Watch this."

Auntie Daz bustled in with a pot of tea
and some homemade biscuits on a tray.

"Here's your tea, Bombassa, dear." She
spoke in a very caring voice. "You need
lots of rest and feeding up. Don't get up,
just stay in bed
and get better."

"I'll try,
Auntie."
Bombassa
sighed and
winked
at Millie.

Millie rolled her eyes and watched as Bombassa dunked his biscuits in the tea and ate them, making crumby drips all over the duvet.

"Ah!" sighed Bombassa. "Just what the doctor ordered!"